KNIGHT'S
CASTLE

BADGER'S
PLACE

GROUNDHOG'
BURROW

SOCCER FIELD

BEAVER'S
POND

PIRATE'S
HAT

Argyle Fox

Marie Letourneau

Tanglewood • Indianapolis, IN

Published by Tanglewood Publishing, Inc.
© 2017 Marie Letourneau

Design by Amy Alick Perich

Tanglewood Publishing, Inc.
1060 N. Capitol Ave., Ste. E-395
Indianapolis, IN 46204
www.tanglewoodbooks.com

Printed in U.S.A.
10 9 8 7 6 5 4 3 2 1
ISBN 978-1-939100-09-2

Library of Congress Cataloging-in-Publication Data

Names: Le Tourneau, Marie, author, illustrator.
Title: Argyle Fox / Marie LeTourneau.
Description: Indianapolis : Tanglewood, 2017. | Summary: When the wind
   interferes with everything grumpy Argyle Fox tries to play outside, his
   mother quietly suggests he think of something made for a windy day.
Identifiers: LCCN 2016026179 (print) | LCCN 2016054141 (ebook) | ISBN
   9781939100092 (hardback) | ISBN 9781939100108
Subjects: | CYAC: Perseverance (Ethics)--Fiction. | Play--Fiction. |
   Foxes--Fiction. | Forest animals--Fiction. | Winds--Fiction. | BISAC:
   JUVENILE FICTION / Animals / Foxes. | JUVENILE FICTION / Social Issues /
   Self-Esteem & Self-Reliance. | JUVENILE FICTION / Sports & Recreation /
   Games. | JUVENILE FICTION / Imagination & Play.
Classification: LCC PZ7.L454 Arg 2017 (print) | LCC PZ7.L454 (ebook) | DDC
   [E]--dc23
LC record available at https://lccn.loc.gov/2016026179

This is Argyle Fox.
He lives in a tree in the forest.

Sometimes in early spring, the
wind whips down the mountainside
and through the trees.

One such day, Argyle told his mother,
"I am going outside to play cards."

"It looks windy out," she replied.
"I think the cards will blow away."

"Hmppph!" said Argyle.

Argyle picked a spot near the old tree stump. For a few minutes, the wind was quiet.

"This is the tallest tower in the entire world!" Argyle cried. But just then...

Wooosh

"Not fair!" said Argyle, and he returned to his tree.

Back at home, Argyle looked
for something else to do.

Found it!

Would it still fit?

Argyle gave it a go.

Indeed it did!

In the forest, Argyle created a web for the world's scariest spider.

"Ta-DA! My web is complete. Beware!" cried Argyle.

"You can't play spider in the wind, Argyle Fox," said the squirrels.

"Beware," replied Argyle with a hiss. "Beware, or I will capture you in my web!"

But just then...

Wooosh

"Phooey!" said Argyle. He decided
to go play pirate near the creek.

"Ahoy, I'm a pirate setting sail
on my ship!" Argyle said.

"You can't play pirate in the wind, Argyle Fox," warned the beavers.

"Arrrg," said Argyle. "I'll make you walk the plank!"

But just then...

"Garrr! Rotten wind!" Argyle cried.
He stomped off toward the meadow.

Ready for the big game, Argyle held his soccer ball.

"I'm the star of the soccer team. I will now kick the winning goal."

"You can't play soccer in the wind, Argyle Fox," said Mr. Badger.

"You'd better watch out, or I will tackle you!" Argyle replied.

Argyle kicked the ball with all his might.

POOOOOT!

But just then...

"Harrumph!" said Argyle as he walked away.
"I didn't really want to play soccer."

On the hillside, Argyle built a castle.

"I am a brave knight, ready to battle the terrible, ferocious, fire-breathing dragon!" declared Argyle.

"You can't play castle in the wind, Argyle Fox."
said the groundhog from his burrow.

"I challenge you to a duel! On your guard!"
said Argyle.

But just then...

Wooosh

"Gah! Rotten, wicked, spiteful wind!
I'm going home!" cried Argyle.

Argyle gathered his things...

...and went home.

"I'm never playing in the wind ever, ever, EVER again!"

"Perhaps if you think for a while, you will figure out something to play in the wind," said Mama Fox.

"No I won't," Argyle grumbled.

"Think, Argyle," Mama Fox said softly as she closed the bedroom door.

BLUE

Argyle thought...

...and thought...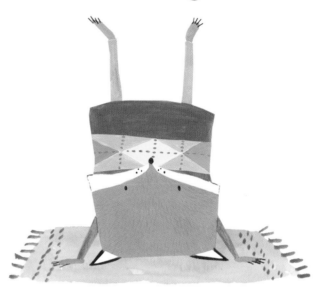

...and looked at his toys...

...and thought some more.

Just then, he knew!

Argyle went straight to work.

He cut,

tied,

knitted,

painted,

and taped.

Finally, it was finished!

TOP SECRET!!

Argyle stood in the meadow, waiting for the wind. His heart pounded with excitement. Would it work? Would he FINALLY be able to play in the wind?

"Huzzah!" cried Argyle. "A kite is the most perfect thing to play in the wind, Mama!"

"Indeed it is," said Mama. "Well done, Argyle. You kept thinking until you knew what to do. You are a clever little fox."

"Thank you, Mama."

FOX

OLD STUMP

ARGYLE'S HOUSE

SPIDER WEB